W9-DFB-056
3 1865 00272 4523

WITHDRAWN

WITHDRAWN

WITHDRAWN

The Adventures of Pettson and Findus
A Ruckus in the Garden

Sven Nordqvist

North
South

It was a lovely spring morning. There were birds singing. The grass
was growing, and insects were flying, so the air was filled with the faint
humming, rustling, burbling murmur of every living thing waking up
again after the winter.

Old man Pettson stood in his vegetable patch, looking at the dirt
and feeling it.

"It's time," he said. "We can plant the vegetables and seed potatoes
today."

Findus the cat was running around scaring beetles.

"You mean *potato seeds*, right?" he said.

"No, *seed potatoes*. If we plant carrot seeds in the soil, carrots will grow.

"And to grow potatoes, you plant potatoes. We call them seed potatoes. For each one we plant, we'll get five to ten new potatoes."

The cat eyed the old man with determination and said, "But I won't like five to ten new potatoes, or carrots either. Couldn't we plant meatballs instead?"

"Well, you can always plant them, but they won't grow," Pettson said.

"But we could try," Findus said.

"Yes, go right ahead, but first we dig and hoe."

Findus ran and fetched one of the meatballs left over from the day before. Pettson turned the vegetable patch and leveled the soil. He sowed the seeds in neat, straight rows—carrots and onions, peas and beans. The cat planted his meatball. Every few minutes he ran over there to see if it had grown.

When there was only one row left to plant, a shrill clucking was heard from over by the house: "Cuh-cuh-cuh-cuh-COME here! He's digging!"

And a moment later, all the hens came running and started scratching in the dirt for worms.

"Oh noooo!" whined Pettson. "I forgot to shut in the hens! You guys can't be out here! You'll ruin everything. You're going to scratch up the seeds!"

But the hens didn't care what the old man said. Worms were their absolute favorite, and wherever someone is digging, it's easy to find worms. No sooner had Pettson chased one hen away than another took her place scratching, so the freshly planted seeds flew every which way. Findus bravely tried to defend his meatball. But even though he roared until he coughed, the hens still nipped at his tail, and in a flash one of them dug up his meatball and swallowed it whole.

"Do I have to shut you in just to keep you out of the vegetable patch?" Pettson scolded. "Come on, let's go get you some sunflower seeds instead."

"We want worms," the hens insisted.

"Then I'll dig you your own spot, where you can eat worms," Pettson said. "Follow me."

Pettson stepped into the chicken run and turned over a patch of dirt. The hens stayed outside the fence.

"There aren't any worms left in there. We ate them all," said Giddy, who was the head hen. She made the decisions.

"Oh yes, there are," Pettson said. "This place is crawling with worms. Come in and you'll see."

"If we go in there, you'll just shut us in so we can't get back out," Giddy said.

Pettson didn't say anything, because that was exactly what he was planning to do. "I won't do that—" he started hesitantly.

Then Findus screamed at the top of his lungs, "THE FOX IS COMING!"

And in one single clucking flutter, all the hens were in. Pettson hurried out and closed the fence.

"Ha-ha! Suckers! Suckers!" Findus laughed. "That's what you get for eating my meatball!"

"You tricked us, Pettson," the chickens clucked.

"You locked us in even though you said you wouldn't."

"But otherwise you'll just mess up everything," Pettson said. "I'll open it again in a few days. If I see any worms, I'll save them for you."

Pettson walked back to the vegetable patch with the cat running ahead of him. They took in the devastation.

"Those darned hens," the old man grunted. "They unplanted it all. Now we have to redo it."

"They unmeatballed it too!" Findus wailed.

Pettson sowed new rows of vegetables, and Findus planted a new meatball. To be on the safe side, he built a sturdy fence around it.

Then it was time for the potato patch. The old man dug trenches, and the cat put the potatoes in. "Well, there we go," Pettson said, breathing hard. "Good to get that done. Now we just have to water and wait."

"You water and I'll wait," Findus suggested.

Findus went out early the next morning to see if his meatball had grown. It hadn't. Quite the contrary. IT WAS GONE! There was only an empty hole! And someone had trampled their beautiful, freshly sowed rows of vegetables. But the potato patch looked even worse.

Everything was all messed up; and there were holes all over the place, and in them NO POTATOES!

Findus ran inside. "Pettson, wake up! My meatball is gone, and every single hole has been unpotatoed!"

"What are you saying, cat? Every single hole unpotatoed?" Pettson hurried outside after the cat.

"Shiver my taters! What is the meaning of this?" Pettson said when he saw the potato patch. "Who did this? I mean, the hens are all locked in. . . . WAIT! THOSE HENS AREN'T ALL LOCKED IN! Listen, you, you, and you! How did you guys get out?"

Three hens were peeking fearfully out from behind a tree.

When Pettson noticed them, they darted straight to the chicken run with the old man after them. But when he opened the door of the henhouse, his hens were all there.

"Can we come out now?" one asked.

"Come out? You've already been out and wrecked the whole potato patch! How did you get out of here?"

The hens clucked:

"We didn't do anything!"

"We were here all night."

"I was asleep."

"I laid some eggs."

"Me too."

"We didn't wreck anything!"

Pettson kept henpecking the hens: "Right, I see. So, apparently my neighbor Gustavsson was over here digging up the potatoes?"

"Pettson, Pettson!" Findus interrupted, jumping onto the old man's shoulder and tapping him on the head with half a potato. "It wasn't them. Look! Whoever did it ate part of the potatoes. Chickens don't eat potatoes."

"Nope," all the hens agreed. "We don't eat potatoes."

"Of course you do," Pettson said, confused.

"But not like this," Findus said. "Look! Big bites. And there are footprints in the dirt. Not the footprints of chickens, but the footprints of unchickens."

"The footprints of unchickens?" the old man snorted. "I'd like to see that."

"We want to see the unchicken footprints too," clucked the hens, and they headed out the door in single file, off to the potato patch. Pettson was the last to arrive. Findus stood in the middle of the flock of hens, carefully studying a footprint and comparing it to his own paw.

"There, you see, Pettson?" Giddy said. "It wasn't us. It was a cow."

"No, a goat," said another of the hens.

"A moose."

"Maybe a frog."

"A Gustavsson."

"No, I know what it was," Pettson said confidently. "It was a—"

"OIIIINK!" they heard from the meadow. "OIIIINK!"

"—a pig. There's Gustavsson with a pig."

Sure enough. The neighbor Gustavsson walked by pulling a pig by a rope.

"She got out last night," Gustavsson called. "I found her in Andersson's potato field. She likes to dig up potatoes."

"Yes, we know," Pettson said. "She was here first and ate her fill."

Gustavsson came closer to look.

"Ooh, that's bad," he muttered. "I'll get you some new potatoes."

"Uh, not to worry," Pettson said. "But it turns out I scolded my chickens for nothing . . . so I guess I might as well let them scratch around here today since it's already messed up. Then I'll plant new potatoes tonight after they go to sleep. You ladies hear that? Scratch all you want now. BUT ONLY IN THE POTATO PATCH. DON'T EVEN LOOK AT THE VEGETABLE PATCH! Promise me!"

"Yeah, we promise," all the hens exclaimed, and immediately started hunting for worms among the clods of dirt.

Pettson set up a makeshift fence between the vegetable patch and the potatoes so the hens wouldn't forget. Findus helped shoo away the hens who didn't know what *promise* meant. He really enjoyed being a guard.

As evening approached, most of the hens returned to the henhouse as usual, but a few remained in the garden, scratching around.

"All right, bedtime, ladies," Pettson called. "The worms are gone. I'm going to plant the potatoes now, and I won't stand for them being dug up again."

"Then you'll be under lock and key for three weeks," Findus said firmly."No! Hush, you!" Pettson said. But it was too late. The hens went nuts, scurrying every which way, clucking and hooting: "He's going to lock us in the henhouse! He's going to trick us again! Bawk-bawk-begawk, don't trust him!"

"Findus!" the old man groaned. "Now look what you did. Why'd you have to say that?"

"I'm sure I haven't said a single word," the cat said, insulted.

"We don't want to be locked in. We're going to stay here all night," Giddy announced.

"But what if the fox comes and gets you," Pettson said.

"It's teeming with foxes outside the fence!" Findus screamed.

"You can't trick us again," Giddy said.

"There's no point henpecking them," Pettson quietly told Findus. "We'll just plant the potatoes and hope for the best."

So Pettson planted potatoes for the second time. Findus planted his third meatball and built an even sturdier fence around it. No one would ever be able to dig it up.

By the time they finished it was almost dark.

"Well, I'm going to bed now. Stay out if you dare," Pettson said. "But no more scratching, promise!"

"Maybe," Giddy said. "We promise. Maybe."

Pettson followed the cat home. He looked worried.

"You know, Findus, I'm a little worried that the fox might come," he said, giving his ear a thoughtful tug.

"I was thinking. . . . I bet you'd find it pretty exciting to stand guard tonight. You see so well in the dark, after all. And when it gets light out, you can wake me up. What do you say?"

The cat's eyes widened. "You want me, a small cat, to chase away foxes? Alone? In the dark of night?"

"No, just stand guard. You can sit in your tree house. And bring a milk pail with a few pebbles in it. And a flashlight. Then if the fox does come, you just rattle the milk pail and shine the flashlight to scare him. And then I'll wake up and come out. Are you brave enough for that?"

"Yeah, of course I'm brave enough. If I sit in the tree house. And have a milk pail. And a flashlight."

Pettson helped Findus get set up in his tree
house. There was no chance a fox would get Findus
up there; plus he had a great view of the whole
yard. The milk pail rattled nicely. To be on the safe
side, they ran a string from the tree house through
Pettson's open bedroom window. When Pettson
went to bed, he would tie it around his big toe. If
Findus pulled on it, the old man would definitely
wake up.

"We're lucky you're so brave, Findus," Pettson said.

"Yes, of course I'm brave," Findus said. "Cats are brave animals."

"They certainly are," Pettson said. "It'll be light again soon. Then you can wake me up. Good night and . . . unsleep well."

Just as Pettson was about to disappear around the corner, Findus yelled: "Are you sure foxes can't climb trees?"

"Yes, yes, I'm sure. But if you're scared, just come back inside with me now."

"No, no. I was just wondering, you know, generally. Good night, old man."

Pettson went in and went to bed. He wasn't that worried about the cat. Findus always did fine. He was more worried about the hens, although it had been a long time since there'd been a fox in the area.

"It would be really unlucky if one happened to show up tonight of all nights."

Findus sat keeping watch alone. He saw the five hens who were holed
up under the bushes. As a cat, he could see quite well even though it was
dark. No fox would come tonight. And *if* one did, then Findus would just
rattle the milk pail, shine the flashlight, tug on the string—rattle, shine,
tug! Rattle, shine, tug! But nothing was going to happen. He would just
sit here and keep watch, and then Pettson would take over.

"No fox will come, no way. Soon it will be light out.
How quiet it is . . . quiet and peaceful.
No sign of any foxes yet.
Twinkle, twinkle, little star,
how I wonder what you are.
Watching over his flock by night . . ."

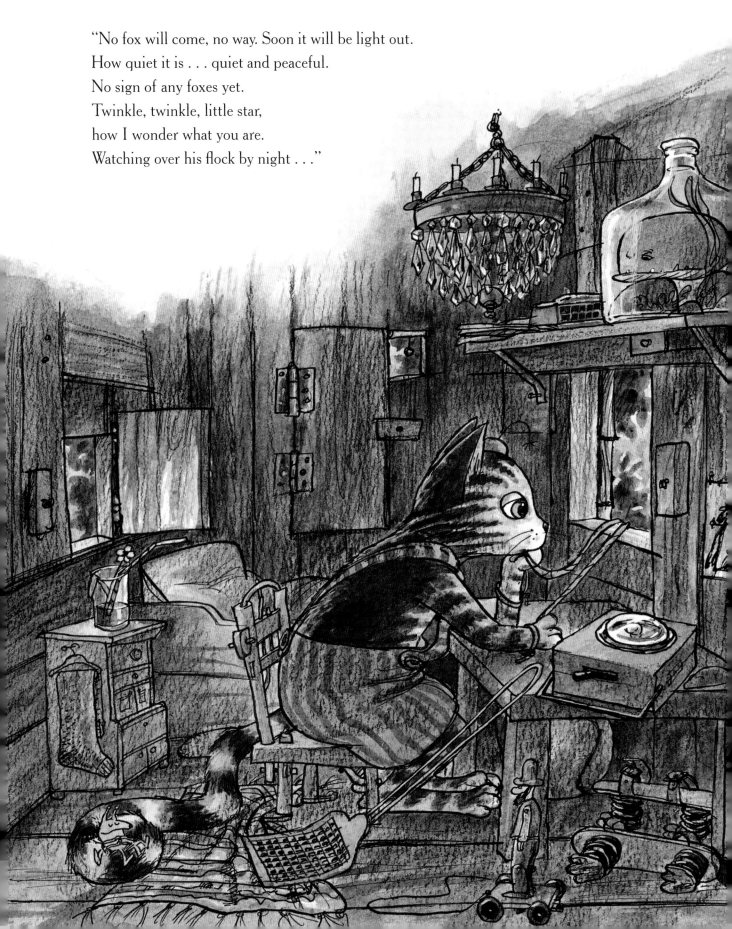

Findus woke with a start. He heard clucking! It wasn't dark anymore? Is it the middle of the next day?! He looked out. HELLLP! RATTLE, RATTLE, SHINE, SHINE, TUG, TUG!

"PETTSON!!! WAKE UP!!! They're trampling my meatball!!!"

Pettson almost flew out the window.

"What is it? Is it the fox? . . . Oh no, not again!!!"

The old man was outside in a flash with his broom in hand. The whole garden was full of cows! At least six of them.

"What are you doing here?" Pettson yelled. "Get out of here. You're destroying the whole garden."

"They're trampling all our worms to death!" cried the hens. But the cows just stood there staring.

"Get away from my flowers! This is my garden, and it's time you got out of here the same way you came in!" Pettson scolded, and started running around driving the cows out, with the help of the chickens and the cat.

But chasing away six cows is no easy matter.

"This isn't working," Pettson panted. "I need to get help. I mean, these are Andersson's cows. He's going to have to help."

"Silly cows! You're silly and nosy," the cat yelled.

"Exactly. Silly and nosy," the old man mumbled, and started walking. But then an idea came into his head, and he stopped suddenly.

"If they're so silly and nosy, maybe we could COAX them out of here. I think I know how."

The cows stood completely still and watched with big eyes as the old man and the cat and the chickens went into the kitchen. The cows walked over to the house to see what was going on. Pettson and the hens came back out looking pleased.

"Ladies and moo-cows," Pettson announced theatrically. "After this wild dance, allow me to present to you: THE ROVING BAG!"

The hens applauded and the cows stared. A paper bag hopped down the kitchen steps. It wandered out into the yard and stopped there. All the cows stared. They'd never seen anything like this before. And now it jingled too, like a cow bell!

The hens scurried over to the bag.

"Whaaaaat bawk-bawk-begawk is that? That's the strangest thing . . . ," they clucked, giving the cows furtive glances.

Overcome with curiosity, the cows jogged toward the bag. As they drew close, it scampered away across the lawn, stopping on the far side. The cows froze, confused. Then the bell jingled and they started moving again, even more eagerly. When they were almost there, the bag ran off up the hill, where it stopped, jumped, and jingled some more. And the cows kept following the bag, and Pettson kept following the cows until they were finally back in the field where they belonged.

Then Pettson fixed their fence. Findus pulled off the bag and ran back to the old man. The cows gaped at them, looking like they had no idea what had just happened, and they didn't either.

"There can't be any more trouble now, I suppose," Pettson said. "I'm going to go to bed now. Tomorrow I'll go around to the neighbors and tell them to mend their fences. Then we'll try to get the garden fixed up again."

"If we just grow my meatball, I think that would be enough. We could plant it in a pot instead," Findus said. "Growing all those vegetables is really hard work."

Be sure to check out the first four books in the series!

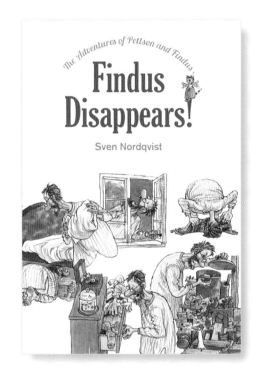

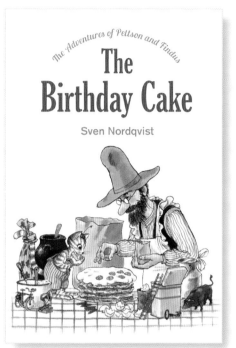